MISSION
CATASTROPHE

Journey Through Ink

Edited By Lynsey Evans

First published in Great Britain in 2024 by:

 Young**Writers**® Est. 1991

Young Writers
Remus House
Coltsfoot Drive
Peterborough
PE2 9BF
Telephone: 01733 890066
Website: www.youngwriters.co.uk

FOREWORD

Young Writers was created in 1991 with the express purpose of promoting and encouraging creative writing. Each competition we create is tailored to the relevant age group, hopefully giving each student the inspiration and incentive to create their own piece of work, whether it's a poem or a short story. We truly believe that seeing their work in print gives students a sense of achievement and pride in their work and themselves.

Mission Catastrophe gave secondary students the opportunity to write about disasters, ranging from world-ending natural events and the consequences of war, to day-to-day mishaps and minor setbacks. These students have explored the consequences of catastrophe big and small, resulting in a varied and entertaining collection of stories.

One of the biggest challenges, aside from facing floods, avoiding avalanches and dealing with lost phones, was to create a mini saga with a beginning, middle and end! Writing with a word constraint allows students to focus on vocabulary choice and takes away the fear of long-form writing, ensuring they get straight to the heart of the story.

The thrilling stories in this collection are sure to set your pulses racing and we're sure you'll agree that Mission Catastrophe has been a success!

CONTENTS

Ramasu Caraballo (12) 50
Jennifer Robinson (12) 51

Gosford Hill School, Kidlington

Ruben Mills (15) 52
Olivia Andrews (13) 53
Helena Gilbert (13) 54
Elizabeth Goodwin (11) 55
Sophie Lewis (13) 56
Arthur Hudson (12) 57

Queen Katharine Academy, Walton

Edyta Hoscilowicz (14) 58
George Holleyoake (14) 59
Matt Kisel (14) 60
Anna Peieira Martins (15) 61
Phoebe Johnson (15) 62
Lucy Crysell (14) 63
Ellie Wesley-Smith (14) 64
Jacob Hale (15) 65
Jakub Barcikowski (14) 66
Taylan Branch (12) 67
Alexandru Stan (14) 68
Fatima Gaye (13) 69
Tendai Mukurunge (13) 70
Leah Knappert (14) 71
Jaden Swaby (15) 72
Andaleeb Hootak (12) 73
Maisey Linnane (12) 74
Eduard Francu (12) 75
Sophie Longland (13) 76
Sofia Alves (14) 77
Stanley Snelling (12) 78
Phoebe Craig (13) 79
Heidi Munton (12) 80
Madison Dickson (14) 81
Lily McCullough (12) 82
Nikita Ignatovic (12) 83
Stevie-Rose Keller (12) 84
Liam Wright (14) 85
Daniela Freimane (14) 86

Roman Levett (13) 87
Zachary Terry (12) 88
Amelia Keeble (14) 89
Jacob Isack (14) 90
Zoha Zahra (12) 91
Gracie Baines (12) 92
Harvey Townsend (14) 93
Summer Turney (12) 94
Mohammed Shamoun (14) 95
Shania Hogan (13) 96
Ebrima Lowe (13) 97
Ubayd Hassan (14) 98
Nyasha Manyeruke (13) 99
Benas Benesevicius (13) 100
Helvan Ali (12) 101
Matas Karčiauskas (13) 102
Kotryna Krutkeviciute (13) 103
Hollie Westgarth (13) 104
Jaela Graham (13) 105
Doulton Coleman (12) 106
Alexandru Ciortan (13) 107
Blake Erskine (13) 108
Latham Fane (15) 109

Raedan Institute, Leicester

Zara Esat (12) 110
Abdullah Motara (12) 111
Ruqayyah Abdurrahman (12) 112
Sumaya Aden (11) 113
Ahmed Taylor (12) 114
Ilyes Boutefennouchet (14) 115
Muhammad Ismael Katib (13) 116
Inaya Chevalier (11) 117
Amaan Chevalier 118
Abdulraheem Katib (12) 119

Sacred Heart High School, Hammersmith

Nicole Kaldas (14) 120
Daisy Inyundo (11) 121
Bethel Kebede (13) 122
Nia Fletcher-Anderson (12) 123

Carmen Zmudzka-Chung (14)	124
Hannah Scully Martin (12)	125
Sofia Carvalho-Hunt (12)	126
Tessa Hogan (14)	127
Eira-Geen Cauilan (12)	128
Anna Rizzato (11)	129
Rosa Barrett (11)	130
Jaya Sharma (12)	131
Lola Pasin (11)	132
Teresa Lo (12)	133
Gabriela Hanna (12)	134

St Margaret's School For Girls, Aberdeen

Olivia Arthur (14)	135
Abigail Onyeakazi (15)	136
Clarissa Iluore (13)	137
Lucinda Kerr (12)	138
Akshaya Allagappan (12)	139
Thejal Senthil (11)	140
Samaira Noor (13)	141
Pippa Stephen (12)	142
Jenny Wang (12)	143
Yazhini Kannan (12)	144
Aditi Krishna (13)	145
Faye Brown (13)	146
Yasmin Wiseman (12)	147
Lucy Cherrie (13)	148

THE MINI SAGAS

Burning

"Mr Prime Minister!"

"What are your commands?"

"The nuclear weapons were launched at our lands!"

"What will we do?" the young reporter asked.

"There's nothing we can do," he responded disappointingly. All of a sudden, the streets were full of uproar and unrest. Some cower while others stand and stare at the bright lights above. This is the end of a once great nation with this Russian demonstration. All those out taking shelter were about to receive a shower of explosions. Big Ben rings one last time before crumbling down. While a child screams once more, "Help me! I'm burning!"

Ruairi Dynes (14)
Aquinas Diocesan Grammar School, Belfast

The End

Two words. The end.
Bombs exploding, planes crashing. Dead bodies.
"Breaking news, four bombs have exploded, causing destruction. 20,000 dead, 6,000 injured."
A thud at the door alarmed me. I hoped it wasn't the postman again, with his letters. It was. Overlooking me, he uttered, "It's about the bombs again,"
I grabbed the letters and strolled out. I didn't care about the bombs. Everything looked the same. Demolished and burned down. I didn't want to look at the letters or anything, and then I turned. Something fell on me. The pain was excruciating. Someone was there. Then it went black.

Meabh Maguire (12)
Aquinas Diocesan Grammar School, Belfast

Met-Quake

In the vibrant city of Metropolis, a series of catastrophic events unfolded. A powerful earthquake struck, leaving many injured. Trees were uprooted and many innocent people were left beneath the rubble. Skyscrapers crumbled and houses couldn't withstand the pressure. Lightbulbs were blown and any electronic device was ripped all the way down to its last circuit. Only the lucky ones survived. Shelters were set up and then destroyed.

Nothing could save Metropolis. Once a vibrant, busy city, it is now a battleground for natural disasters. Once a fantastic city to live in, it is now a desolate city where rubble goes to rot.

Oliver McNulty (13)
Aquinas Diocesan Grammar School, Belfast

The Collision

Two minutes until impact.
I desperately banged the keys on the flashing computer, trying with all my might to avoid a collision.
One minute until impact.
I could hear them screaming.
Thirty seconds until impact.
I wouldn't give up, not now.
Fifteen seconds unt...
I shut the machine off. I couldn't bear thinking it was over, not after everything I had been through. And then, finally, I did it! But it was too late. The giant silhouette of the gargantuan moon engulfed all of the light in the room with its pitch-black shadow. There was no hope. It was over.

Leo Rooney (12)
Aquinas Diocesan Grammar School, Belfast

Another Problem

Time: 0800.

I heard in my head, "Missile launch detected."

Then everything went wrong. I got out of bed to a scream, breaking the silence of the sterile city.

I sprinted outside to the horrifying sight of a pilot being ripped apart by a pack of coyotes. A coyote turned its head to me. It barked and snarled. I backed away. The pack all turned. I started running backwards and the chase began. I sprinted towards an office. The warning sirens started shrieking again.

"Oh no," I said, "another problem."

I saw a light in the sky. A nuke.

John O'Hare (12)
Aquinas Diocesan Grammar School, Belfast

Going Down

"We're just having some minor turbulence."
I took no notice and kept reading my magazine. Suddenly, everything went dark. A huge explosion shook the plane. Startled, I looked left and saw a flaming engine. By now panic had enveloped the other passengers. I could feel the plane dipping. I needed to get to the cockpit before it was too late. I shoved through the crowd, the plane falling even faster. I bolted through the cockpit doors, only to see two empty seats. But what really scared me was what I saw next. "Oh no." It was a nuclear power plant...

Aonghus Lennon (14)
Aquinas Diocesan Grammar School, Belfast

Why Me?

The sky was ablaze with the fire of a thousand cannons as the screams of innocent people echoed throughout the city. Bullets whistled as they flew past and the ground shook violently under the relentless armies marching determinedly through the once-calm city. Mum called me to the kitchen, "Mike!" she screamed out. I sprinted down, but as I reached the kitchen door, something had happened. It was only me, no one else. No bombs, no loud marching, nobody... what had happened? Why was I suddenly alone? Why was I the only one left in this city? Why not them? Why me?

Abbie Dolaghan Taylor (13)
Aquinas Diocesan Grammar School, Belfast

Lights Off

All the lights went off. The ground started shaking.
Crash!
One of the vases fell off the table. I got on my knees and crawled under the table. I looked around me to try to spot Mum and Sarah. That's when I saw Mum, running through the back door. Where was she going? And why wasn't Sarah with her?
The banister snapped in half! I stumbled to the cupboard under the stairs to grab the earthquake kit. But it wasn't there! It was there last week! That's when I saw Sarah. She was running down the stairs. But something was chasing her...

Rose Sands (13)
Aquinas Diocesan Grammar School, Belfast

Desert Disaster

I didn't mean for this to happen. Everything started as a normal day in Dubai UAE, one of the biggest oil production towns. I was doing my usual job of examining data but then my eyes rolled over something that would later be devastating if not patched up. It was a colossal cavity that held poisonous gasses that could kill potentially all of the population of Dubai. A loud alarm, that indicated the drilling process was underway, beeped. Then, the noise of the huge drill erupted. The gas was slowly seeping up to the surface. My last thought was, *oh god...*

Harshil Santhoshkumar (13)
Aquinas Diocesan Grammar School, Belfast

Tsunami

The wind whipped and whistled by. Telephone and electrical lines toppled like dominoes, the rain fell like bullets from up above. We watched from the uppermost window of the apartment block. The bottom four floors were submerged, and all belongings were gone in the murky waters. The beach seemed to dry up, the waters pulling away revealing... square waves? But then in the distance, a looming shadow was growing bigger and darker, snatching up boats and debris. My gut was churning as I realised this was not just a storm but a tsunami. All of a sudden, it was upon us.

Shane Bell (14)
Aquinas Diocesan Grammar School, Belfast

The Crash

The plane crashed into the jungle. I was excited to go to the beautiful Barbados, but this was different. I heard gunshots in the distance getting closer.

I started running, running like the wind. I could've run for hours, weeks, months. I didn't know. Suddenly, I tripped and fell. It went black. Then, I woke up.

"Ready to go to Barbados?" asked Dad.

"I don't want to go," I said.

On the plane, I felt sick with fear. There was a jolt, and suddenly, the plane was falling out of the sky. My nightmare had come true.

Saoirse Morelli (13)
Aquinas Diocesan Grammar School, Belfast

Earth's End

Catapulting closer, at lightning speed like a shooting star. The Earth trembled, everyone frozen like a statue. The brightness blinded everybody. It was inevitable. We all gazed up, accepting our fate. Inching closer, the heat began to hit us all. *Thud!* It was all over. I could no longer feel a solitary thing. The bright white light flashed before my eyes. I tried desperately to move, but it was like lighting a fire in the ocean. My body began to rise, directly toward the white light. It was over, not only for me but for all of us.

Rory Armstrong (14)
Aquinas Diocesan Grammar School, Belfast

Silence

That's when it hit. No one knows the complete isolation an astronaut feels. Silence, utter silence. The wave of heat hit me. The explosion came from the now charred and blackened Earth. I tried, I really tried. But to no avail. It seemed as though the vacuum of space in Earth's orbit occupied me and my ship. I screamed out in anger but I knew the pointlessness of it. I struck out in anger, antagonised by the slowness of my movements. There was no one left. I let myself go, opening my helmet and floating away. A dead race finished.

Daniel Kelly (14)
Aquinas Diocesan Grammar School, Belfast

Earth Shatter

We thought it was just like any old earthquake. This wasn't normal. As the buildings were engulfed in smoke, the whine of sirens rang out in my ear. The thin road was being torn apart like it was no more than a piece of paper. I ran out just to grip the doorframe again as the gap was far closer to my house than anticipated, and thankfully I did, as at that moment, my house was catapulted into the vastness of space. It was sort of peaceful out there, seeing the Earth's core reveal itself after being enshrouded in rock and darkness.

Fionn Johnston (14)
Aquinas Diocesan Grammar School, Belfast

The Day It All Changed

The smoke was choking me and I thought my world might explode. It began when my country got bombed by Russia. They were looking for something we didn't know we had. Flaming bodies, burning bodies, burning buildings and a blown-up lifestyle. I saw a man then I was sprinting and he was too. I felt acid burning in my throat, I kept going until I couldn't anymore, because the ground from underneath my feet was gone. I was falling, I let out a scream before landing in a pit of lava. I felt each limb melt and then it all went dark.

Aoibhe Waring (13)
Aquinas Diocesan Grammar School, Belfast

Real-Life Nightmare

Bang!

I could hear ringing in my ears.

Thud!

The sound of my fists banging on the walls. The room was dark and murky. The floor was damp. My head was swimming in pain. I felt as if I had been stabbed, or had I been? My hand was shaking as I placed it on my stomach. It was covered in blood. It all came back to me. Everyone I had ever known or loved was gone. It felt like a horrible nightmare, but I couldn't wake up. It had actually happened. It was all my fault. Everything was my fault!

Tess Gillen (13)

Aquinas Diocesan Grammar School, Belfast

Hell Time In Belfast

Boom! The rock lay dormant on our sofa and, through the hole in our roof, I could see a glimpse of my death. Cosmic entity born only from pure hatred for the universe's oasis, destroying all in its path. With nothing else to do, I ran, I didn't know where to, but I felt like it didn't matter that my last moments would be wasted. I shuddered with the horror that was wrought with every glance. The sky was red and was filled with maroon. Streets were filled with bodies and flesh.

Vincent Egan (14)
Aquinas Diocesan Grammar School, Belfast

The Final

It was the final in my running tournament. After practising the night before I was pumped and when I was walking back in I tripped on the cat! I fell and hurt my ankle! I didn't tell my mum as I was determined to run the final. I woke up the next morning my ankle still in agony but still determined. I got there and ran a quarter then fainted because of the pain! I woke up lying in the hospital, it turned out I had sprained my ankle and broken my leg! I had never been more devastated before.

Katie Harrison (13)
Aquinas Diocesan Grammar School, Belfast

The Drive

"Sooner or later, you're gonna have to learn," Dad jeered as he left the car. My 16th birthday had just passed, so driving talks tend to dominate our conversations. He uses the pump to fuel the car, which oddly begins levitating. I gasp and turn, where I encounter a pale green, wrinkled creature staring through the driver's window. Horrified, I look down in search of Dad, only to see his limp body being dragged behind the convenience store. They surround the car. Impulsively, I dart into the driver's seat, turn on the engine and speed off into the sky.

Maria Akeredolu (16)
Bacon's College, Rotherhithe

The Last Summer

I woke up. The past events swarmed around me. But I couldn't understand. Had I caused all this? I... I couldn't remember. Only the vibrant tones of death and destruction roamed in my brain while I saw what was left of humanity and life die before me. Suddenly, a feeling came to me. It was like... a thought, but in a way where I was positive, one hundred percent positive this was true. No matter the context, what I felt was appalling. I was the last living thing on Earth.

Mila Spence (11)
Bacon's College, Rotherhithe

Escaping From The Plagued Island

The plague has now spread! Everyone has been infected by this plague. Am I the only one who was not infected? I need to escape, yet how? There is an escape, but this escape will be tricky to do. I'll need resources and food, but there are many obstacles in the way. I'll need all the strength I have to overcome them.

Maryam Kazi-Hussen (12)

Bacon's College, Rotherhithe

Scientific Report

Report by Dr Martin
Date 19/10/2038
We have done days worth of research and so far nothing
has been considered useful. Strangely, only those between
the ages of 15-60 have been targeted by the parasite. We
have found that the parasite can be located in the cranium
and tends to wrap around the brain, leading to headaches,
double vision, nausea and vomiting, dizziness and ringing in
the ears. Victims of the parasite are currently being tested
for more side effects. Our research will continue and
hopefully, we will get some positive results in the near
future.

Lacey Clark (13)
Barlby High School, Barlby

The Chaos Of The War

We could hear the screams from the town centre. World War Three had begun. Streams of people running underground, police everywhere. We were in the underground train station. The sound of bombs and shouting filled the room with negative energy. An hour passed before we were given the all-clear. When I saw the state of our hometown I wanted to stay underground. Dust and debris covered the town with broken shards of glass and the bodies of people who didn't make it. We got rehomed into shelters. A group of people and I cried about our losses.

Aisha Bell (13)
Barlby High School, Barlby

Betrayal Like Poison

"Listen! We have a cure and a vaccine! Meet at Terrace of the Last!" exclaimed a loud female voice from the television. The rebels were the only thing standing between enemy zombies and a complete apocalypse.

I dashed out of the house and breathed a sigh of relief as I saw Connie, my best friend, and also the person that was holding the vaccine and the cure. They were tinted a bright turquoise colour.

"We'll poison the humans!" Connie whispered to a hooded figure. I leapt out, knocking the serums from their grip. They clinked onto the floor.

"You wish, traitors!"

Amal Abdullah (12)
Barton Court Grammar School, Canterbury

The Great Death

How did this even come to pass? All I ever asked for was the responsibility and the joy a German shepherd would give me. But no, wherever I go, trouble follows. I mean, how was some fourteen-year-old meant to know a bomber would come in the form of a delivery guy?

Oh well, I was going to die anyway.

The bombs had gone off simultaneously, making this more dangerous.

Well goodbye, I'm dead. Unless...

No, don't you dare.

Why not? Just press that *'Unleash The Monster'*.

Great. A girl about my age entered! Maybe it wasn't over?

Rumble...

Mosinoluwa Sosan (11)

Barton Court Grammar School, Canterbury

The Unexpected Visitors

I woke with a start. There was thunder, a bad omen. Carefully exiting my creaking bed, I gently woke my twin sister, Zara, alert of how grumpy she could be. We had slept in (unusual), another bad omen. My mind immediately raced to my parents. Why hadn't they woke us up for school? Suddenly, the door opened to reveal uncanny-looking creatures possessing muddy brown eyes and sea-green skin. Although they had a sluggish, unfamiliar gait, they seemed to get quicker every ticking second.

"Help!" Zara screamed.

No one answered. Why were they here? Were we the only ones left?

Zoe Oguntola (11)
Barton Court Grammar School, Canterbury

The Crack Of History

"Emergency! Evacuation plan activating."
The crack grew as the everlasting days went by. But today was different. The village was gathered by the crack in the mountain. I looked at a sign. It said that the King of Dragons lived there. The gargantuan, natural landmark shook and then a blast of icy wind was bestowed on us. Everyone was frozen, apart from me. There it was, the beast. It was white like snow, red like blood and had tusks that could pierce anything. It rose from the mountain and its wings spread like wildfire. It flapped its wings, and I vanished.

Ivan Waller (11)
Barton Court Grammar School, Canterbury

All Alone

I don't know what has happened to the world. Since the EMP everyone's descended into madness. My own family abandoned me and left me to die at home as they fled for good, forever. But nothing works, the electricity is down, computers are down, everything and almost everyone is dead! I left my house once, quickly realising the severity of the violence and chaos and ran for cover. Still, the deafening gunshots and fearful streets never cease. More and more gangs close in, taking everything we own and all I can do is wait for the relief of death. Alone, helpless.

Rachel Lawrence (12)
Barton Court Grammar School, Canterbury

The Suffering

It has been days since the nuclear blast, and the only survivors are dying of rampaging cancer or mutating diseases that cause bodies to shrivel and become mindless unkillable spawn of Satan. If you stay away from said monsters you can be sure The Mighty One will find you. A beast of titanic proportions with six arms and no legs, only a tail. He can summon dark tentacles from surrounding matter and emit radiation. His grotesque face is reminiscent of the human it once was. He can only be erased by the dark arts and witchcraft. Trust me, we won't last long.

Samko Biagi (11)
Barton Court Grammar School, Canterbury

Hope?

In the aftermath of chaos, humanity stood divided. Some, broken by despair, resigned themselves to their fate. Others fueled by resilience, refused to yield. Amidst rubble and ruin a whisper of hope emerged. United by a shared determination they forged ahead, rebuilding what was lost. Each brick laid, each hand extended. A testament to the indomitable spirit of mankind. The catastrophe may have shattered their world, but it could not break their will. In the face of adversity, they chose not to surrender, but to rise, stronger and more united than ever before.

Rumaisah Ahmed (12)
Barton Court Grammar School, Canterbury

Here Comes The Sun

"Why is everything such a catastrophe?" Everything went dark.

Suddenly the lights went out, but all I could see was a roaring flame coming towards me...

The next thing I knew, I was on the ground with flames surrounding me.

I rushed around the village to see if everyone was okay. I kept saying to myself, "Is this the end of the world? If it is, why does it happen to me?"

Suddenly, I was surrounded by magma to the point that I turned hopeless.

It came closer and closer to the point where I was done. I was dead.

Amelia Hughes (12)
Barton Court Grammar School, Canterbury

The Message

My phone lit up with an eerie glow as a spine-chilling message flashed across it, 'I know what you did'. The words taunted me, a numbing grip touching me. Who would possibly know my darkest secret? Panic set in as I frantically searched for the sender, but the message had no trace as if it had come from beyond the grave. The room grew colder, the shadows stretching menacingly towards me. I felt like I was being watched, like a predator stalking prey. The message had a deathly grip on my mind, leaving me haunted by the extensive unknown.

Manha Ahmad (12)
Barton Court Grammar School, Canterbury

The Last Life Remaining

No, no, no, no! Death had caught up to me. The screams of people rang through my ears. I ran with speed. The true opponent wasn't the raging fire that flocked around the city like a raging bull looking for prey. I ran, wondering not of my surroundings. Then, the true opponent appeared: fear. A god that showed up at times of trouble. He controlled as a master commands his wishes to a puppet, a mere slave. I stopped, feet trembling and accepted the inevitable death. But a person stretched his hand out to me, an array of light in darkness.

Ara Sobowale (12)
Barton Court Grammar School, Canterbury

The Sun Too Soon

They said the sun was getting closer, but I thought not. It was January, but every day was getting hotter as if it were the middle of summer. The sun seemed to draw closer each day, but this was not meant to happen. Night never fell. Something was weird. Odd. I decided to go outside, and there it was: the sun. Miles away from us, but here. I knew that very second, we were all hours away from death. I went straight upstairs and woke everyone for the last time; it was the end of humanity. Midnight struck, and everything went black...

Elsie Brown (12)
Barton Court Grammar School, Canterbury

Death Of Playtime Co.

I was en route to the safehouse, stressing. I knew he was following me; it was just a matter of when he got me. I tried but failed, nonetheless. Everyone in town knew my name; I was a fugitive. Nobody understood why; they just knew I was no good. But if they'd investigated my history, they'd have seen sweet, innocent me caught up in something sinister. Every experiment, test and interview all led to this point. I unlocked the door to find guns waiting. Shots rang out. Goodbye, Playtime Co. The torture was over. He was dead.

Brooke Bolton (14)
Barton Court Grammar School, Canterbury

The Disappearance

I walked home happily. I couldn't wait to see my family again. I had only been away for one night, but it felt like ages. Overnight in the wilderness was scary but fun. There was no one about, which was weird. But there was probably something important on.

As I stepped into my house, I heard no one, saw no one. They said they would be happily waiting for me when I got home. Why would they lie? I cautiously took a step into my living room. I picked up the remote, and it turned on the TV: static. *Am I the only one?*

Iris Fitzgerald (11)

Barton Court Grammar School, Canterbury

Spy Mission Asunder

I was having the worst day ever. I didn't mean for the criminal to get away. Let's start from the beginning.
I was called into the office for a mission with my sister. We had been in the CIA for two years, I've ruined it all for us. We were supposed to guard the criminal and find out stuff about him but because I didn't check our security, the criminal broke out. The level of problem I am in right now is more than World War One and World War Two joined together. What's going to happen to me now? Doomed.

Syntyche Oyedele (12)
Barton Court Grammar School, Canterbury

Interdimensional Resurgence: Dr Emily Carter's Last Stand...

In a world ravaged by chaos, survivors fought to stay alive. Cities lay in ruins, consumed by an unknown force. As the sun set on humanity, hope emerged. Doctor Emily Carter, a brilliant scientist, discovered a portal to another dimension. With time running out, she gathered a team. They stepped through, entering a realm of advanced technology and alien beings. Together, they fought impending doom, determined to save their friends, families and above all, their world...

Theo Pereira (11)
Barton Court Grammar School, Canterbury

Day Of Disaster

I woke up, but no one was there. I was pretty confused but brushed it off. Stupid mistake! Walking around, the fear of zombies nearby. It would've been better than what I saw. My best friend. Her body limp. Lifeless.

"No!" I screamed out in anger. "This is a joke! It's a joke!"

Click. Click. Click.

A trigger. Someone with a gun.

Bang. Bang. Bang.

Footsteps. My heart was in my throat. I wanted to scream, cry, run away. But I was frozen. Suddenly, a masked man appeared... tall, skinny. He pulled the trigger. I was gone forever without reason. Why?

Mollie White (12)

Carrick Academy, Maybole

Winners And Losers

He wakes up, checks his phone to find two texts: 'You're fired!' and 'We're breaking up!' Montague gets up, stubs his toe. On hearing a bang, he runs outside. There's an excavator destroying his old Mustang. The bank calls, "We're repossessing your house!" From across the street, his mother shouts, "Things happen for a reason!" A random man kicks his cat. He sighs and goes to the shop with his last £5. He buys a scratchcard - top prize, a million. He scratches. He wins. He's rich.
A gust of wind sweeps the ticket high up into the air. Gone!

Noah McPhee (13)
Carrick Academy, Maybole

Safe Or Not So Safe?

Lying in my bed, I feel the ground shake. Looking out the window, I see helicopters, tanks and cars. I wonder to myself whether World War Three is actually happening. Right now. Hiding in my basement I hear the loudest bang - the clock tower next to my house is being bombed. I panic because I don't want my house destroyed too. I slowly sneak outside. Running as far as I can, I know I must escape this catastrophe no matter what it is. Forever.

Making it to the woods, I find safety. "Argh... Where did that rabid dog come from?"

Lyle Leck (13)
Carrick Academy, Maybole

Bad Luck

I dozed back off after the alarm only to wake up to the smell of smoke. My breakfast. I jumped up to take the bacon out of the pan only to burn myself. Big blister. I hurried to work with a burned bacon sandwich only for a street dog to leap up unexpectedly and yank it out of my hand. There goes breakfast! Hungry tummy. Okay, okay... coffee at work to calm me down. I stretched up on tiptoes for the coffee beans from the top shelf only for them to flood all over my feet.
Just my goddamn luck!

Fraya Wiseman (13)
Carrick Academy, Maybole

Boxed In

I wake up and I'm in a metal box of some kind. The scent of metal and sweat clouds my senses before the panic overwhelms me. I look around, but as soon as I try to stand the box shakes and knocks me back to the ground. I yell and yell but it's as if I'm a thousand miles away from any humanity. Tears well up in my eyes, I give up and lie down. When I accept that I'm trapped the box stops and shakes for a minute. Then the top opens, the bright light making my eyes close.

Payton Donnachie (13)
Carrick Academy, Maybole

Elements

28th February, 3000. Doomsday.
The world panicked when civilians noticed Water acting strangely. Tsunamis fiercely crashed while whirlpools submerged first-rate sailors. Countless were evacuated into claustrophobic bunkers. Then, Fire arrived. The ground smoked, volcanoes spewed mountains of lava. Populations dwindled as problems increased. Earth followed, plants wilted and rockfalls swept across the remains of the once captivating landscape. Survivors became paranoid, dreading when the wind would thrash upon them, and it soon struck. Tornadoes formed, lashing out at every remnant of life, and forceful winds carried debris everywhere. Then... peace. But none to enjoy it. Earth rested as a decaying wasteland.

Hoi Ching Lam (12)
Currie Community High School, Currie

The Boom!

Boom!

"Hahaha, I won!" I said to my friend. "You'll never beat me, you're really bad at this!"

He rolled his eyes, "I demand a rematch!" he replied.

He wasn't the losing sort of person, so I thought one more time of me winning wouldn't matter.

"Sure!" I said and started to set the game back up.

Boom!

"I don't think that was the game, was it you?" I asked him.

"No, what do you think I am, a bomb?"

"Okay, fine, what do you think it was?"

"Breaking news! A nuclear bomb has been set off! Evacuate now!"

Hannah Campbell (13)

Currie Community High School, Currie

The Bunker

The TV flashed. Ruins were displayed on the screen. Alcatraz prisons blew up. 50 convicts escaped. You're not safe. The TV flickered. Millie ran. She ran for hours, till she reached the safest place known. She entered the password. Millie was swallowed into darkness. She saw the light again. A lantern was hanging from the roof. Millie waited. Hours later, she heard the door open. Footsteps echoed on the path. Someone appeared. Liam. They waited in darkness. They'd survive. The door opened. They were safe. Convicts were still on the run, yet they didn't need to be worried. The bunker kept them safe.

Elissa Savidge (13)
Currie Community High School, Currie

The End

I wake up to screaming reverberating around the town. The radio states there is a new global pandemic. Trepidation strikes. I hear my neighbour screaming with dread as some sort of zombie creature crawls into their home laughing. The creature looks like a human, but its skin is peeling away to reveal scaly flesh around its body. Suddenly, I hear a huge bang from next door and then a screech of laughter as my neighbour, no longer the same, stumbles out of their house. Is this the end of humankind? What's to come for us? They are here goodbye...

Ellis Brannan (12)
Currie Community High School, Currie

Dancing With Death

We are dropping dead like flies, some of us have been dancing with death for weeks now. Nothing is the same anymore. This dancing plague sweeps across France and Rome, killing hundreds of thousands, whether they're men, women or children. Death toys us around like puppets on stage being forced to dance for weeks with no break. Unlike actors we don't get applause at the end of our show, instead, we drop, never to show up again. Why now? Why us? What did we do wrong that we should be punished most cruelly? We wait for sweet relief.

Mia Elizabeth Hogg (12)
Currie Community High School, Currie

The Catastrophic Disaster

It was a bright morning. But suddenly the sky changed. It was a bright yellow. Suddenly, a scary red tornado emerged. I could hear screaming in the distance. There were animals, creatures falling. Then it was over my house. We locked all the doors, but that was not enough. I hid under my bed. Then I heard my mum scream from downstairs. The hairs on my back prickled up. It passed. I sprinted down the stairs. There was my mum covered in blood, dead. I looked outside for anything. Nothing was there. I went back inside and there it was.

Scott Matthew
Currie Community High School, Currie

The Rain

It was a casual peaceful day. I was at a picnic with my parents and my cousin, we were eating pancakes, waffles and sausages. It was good, really good. Then I decided to look up at the sky and the sky looked green. That was very strange. I told my mum about it and she said, "Son it's only just green, I've seen worse in my days."
I looked at my cousin and she looked at me. We knew what to do. We hid under a shelter and watched my parents burn. It was the worst day of my life.

Ramasu Caraballo (12)
Currie Community High School, Currie

Untitled

I was having a nightmare and suddenly I woke up. I checked the time, it was 4:37 and I just lay there. I thought about the classes I had that day, oh I had the most important test! It was one that I had to get an A on, otherwise I would have to retake the whole year! So I got up and sat at my desk thinking, *why did I leave my revision till the last minute?* I stayed there and studied so hard. I looked up and saw the time, it was 8:47! School started 17 minutes ago!

Jennifer Robinson (12)
Currie Community High School, Currie

Dawn

Tick.
The day begins, sun rising, lazily charting its way across the sky.
Tick.
The city wakes, blinking its eyes at the brightness of the new dawn.
Boom.
The brightness surges, a star born across the horizon, the conflagration starts, an inescapable light, a fire that burns the earth and bursts forth like a wave. Red and orange and brutal, blinding white, until nothing's left but black.
The smoke rises from the rubble.
A hacking cough breaks the silence.
A figure staggers through the smoke.
They hold a lantern, a sun, a hope, a promise for this new day.

Ruben Mills (15)
Gosford Hill School, Kidlington

My Last Goodbye

The news called it an 'airborne anomaly'. I called it the end. The spores, invisible assassins, turned lungs into crystals. Gasping breaths echoed in the sterile halls as the healthy became infected overnight. Laughter, replaced by rattling coughs, died with each sunrise. Now, the silence was deafening. I watched a single spore drift, a harbinger of death, in the dust-filled shaft of sunlight that pierced my boarded-up haven. I think I'm the last one left; I can't tell. Going outside isn't safe anymore. Nothing is safe anymore. I'm running out of food; this may be my last entry. Farewell.

Olivia Andrews (13)
Gosford Hill School, Kidlington

Push The Button

It wasn't a dark and stormy night, but it should've been.
The masterwork of taking over the world was finished. Ansel
got up from his desk and watched the sunrise. Today he
would let his plan loose.

The maelstrom of bots and viruses that he would set free on
the internet made him cackle uncontrollably.

Nobody would be able to use the internet, causing violence
between all the people. Everybody would be confused,
flustered and unable to work.

Ansel didn't like the new age of technology so he decided to
stop it.

If he didn't need the computers, nobody did.

Helena Gilbert (13)
Gosford Hill School, Kidlington

The Annual Purge

9 o'clock in the evening. I was texting a friend when the alert popped up on my phone: 'Blue alert. This is not a test. This is the commencing of the annual purge'.
My friend texted, 'Did you get that too?'
I was going to reply when an abrupt bang caught my attention, so I looked outside to see all hell had broken loose.
Bombs and gunshots were flying left and right. Then I heard a small ticking behind me.
I jumped out of the window just as my house exploded: I almost felt a tear when I noticed from behind the tree. Maria.

Elizabeth Goodwin (11)
Gosford Hill School, Kidlington

The End Of The World

That night, the bombs fell like rain; the kind of rain that pierces your skin with tiny, frozen bullets. But the bombs were more destructive than that. They crushed your bones, burying you alive. Death would carry your soul deep into his lair. There were no survivors, you were destined to die.

A group of friends huddled together amongst the rubble. They would never forget the horrors they had seen, not that they had much longer to remember. The bombs were almost upon them.

That was how they stayed, a group of children, waiting for the end of the world.

Sophie Lewis (13)
Gosford Hill School, Kidlington

Catastrophe

I was running. Or was I dead? It didn't matter, as my legs pressed on, my weary eyes helplessly searching for something, anything. But that something never came. I was only met by smouldering flames, desperate to suck the slowly dying life out of me.

The whole town was ablaze, the marina, chaos. Sailboats desperately tried to flee the inferno of coppery fire before it entangled them. The dying sun staggered into the scarlet horizon, and tears pooled up in my sore eyes. I collapsed, flames roaring up around me like lions engulfing me one last time.

Arthur Hudson (12)
Gosford Hill School, Kidlington

Lights Out

Radio: "*A power outage has affected the whole country. Keep safe during the night as the government tries to solve the problem.*"

The house is engulfed in darkness, the only light source being candles that were placed when we found out there was no fixing the lights. We know about what dangers a pitch-black night can deliver. Kidnappers... Murderers...

We're keeping the radio in the living room, getting up to date on any vital information.

When it's day, the sun grants light, although people are still terrified. It's still not solved... people are dying out there, especially at night.

Edyta Hoscilowicz (14)
Queen Katharine Academy, Walton

The Martian War

They came from the clouds. The Martians. Spinning plates encased them in their descent onto our Great Britain. However, these monstrous flying machines weren't their only entry. From the very earth we stand on came a great rumbling and from that, the quadrupods. These walking behemoths emitted an ear-piercing screech while simultaneously beaming rays of light that disintegrated all they touched. The world itself had fallen to the might of the Martians, with our cities vaporising under the immense heat of their engines. Our armies had fallen. Our countries had fallen. Our world had fallen. This was our extinction.

George Holleyoake (14)
Queen Katharine Academy, Walton

Zombie Outbreak

"Breaking news: the Prime Minister has declared an emergency state lockdown. A plane from the United States of America has crashed, releasing zombies outside in London."
Panic spread across the UK. Zombies broke down doors. Explosions were heard across London. How would we survive this? Resources were low, water was low. This was a catastrophe.
I was hiding in a flat. I broke into tears. Millions of zombies broke into the apartment. The lights flickered. I tearfully grabbed the metal bat.
"Breaking news: all of London is currently infected. We think London will be wiped out."

Matt Kisel (14)
Queen Katharine Academy, Walton

Untitled

In the midst of the pouring rain, panic surged as their car skidded off the road, crashing into the muddy embankment. Flipping upside down, the vehicle's roof cracked open like an eggshell. Trapped with the driver's side door wedged in the mud, he found his sister injured inside, blood trickling from her mouth. Suddenly, a shadowy figure appeared, seizing his sister. Despite her struggles, the main character watched helplessly as his sister fell silent, lifeless. With dread coursing through his veins, he knew he was in a nightmare. The assailant fled into the darkness, leaving him to face the unknown.

Anna Peieira Martins (15)
Queen Katharine Academy, Walton

Life Or Death

You watch the droplets race each other, fighting for the win, stationary in a traffic jam, running late for work. You hear the violent pattering creep into your brain. You need to keep focused, pushing your foot on the pedal. Continuous voices in your head shouting at you to stop immediately. You're not thinking straight. You accelerate at full speed and don't stop. The glass panes shatter, then nothing. Deafening silence fills the city until... endless sirens scream out into the distance, and echoing cries of innocent children break the silence as the world starts to fall apart. Will you survive?

Phoebe Johnson (15)
Queen Katharine Academy, Walton

The Ice Age Is Back?

As the nights get colder, scientists bring more and more creatures back from the ice age.
As the next day arrives, I look out of my window and scream.
My mum comes up and says, "What is wrong, Lucy?"
I say, "There is a sabretooth outside our house!"
My brother says, "You are probably lying, Sis."
I shout angrily, *"No! I am not!"*
My brother and mum look out the window, shocked.
I say, "I told you both I wasn't lying!"
My mum and brother say, "We are so sorry."
I accept their apology.

Lucy Crysell (14)
Queen Katharine Academy, Walton

Hazbin Hotel Vs Heaven

Extermination day. A normal year for the sinners. But wait...
something's not right. Angels are dropping like flies. This
isn't right. Sinners aren't meant to kill. They are the ones
who are meant to be killed. Adam isn't going for any other
sinners. Just one in particular. Adam was caught up trying to
kill Charlie and her people. Only Luke saw what was going
to happen. Luke ran quicker than before. Niffty, Charlie's
housewife, had an angelic weapon and was heading toward
Adam. Luke pushed Adam out of the way, getting himself
killed. This was the first time Heaven ever lost.

Ellie Wesley-Smith (14)
Queen Katharine Academy, Walton

Five Nights At Freddy's, Dark Return

The restaurant was abandoned. It had been frozen in time for a long time. Before it was shut there was a massacre. Six children were pronounced missing not long after visiting Freddy Fazbear's Pizzeria. After an investigation, it was found that the owner had kidnapped and murdered the children. During the investigation, the owner confessed to stuffing the bodies of the children inside the animatronics. A team was sent to capture the animatronics but they were all missing. A couple of years passed and the owner of the pizzeria was released but the animatronics also returned to start killing.

Jacob Hale (15)
Queen Katharine Academy, Walton

The Great Collapse

It was on the 9th of November that the world would change. In the city of Dubai, 8am, the wind was thrusting through the air, people were travelling across the city and aeroplanes soaring across the bright blue sky. Then *boom!* A sudden burst of flames spread like wildfire up on the higher floors. Out of the smoke, two masked individuals were escaping the big scene, using parachutes as a getaway. News quickly broke out of the situation, both masked figures were caught, but the damage was already done. The Burj Khalifa soon collapsed upon itself, destroyed, leaving nothing but ash.

Jakub Barcikowski (14)
Queen Katharine Academy, Walton

Coming Back

He sat in his room, bored as always, playing PlayStation until his mum stormed in panicked. He'd never seen her like this. His eyes widened when she showed him the newspaper without saying a word. Uncle Rick was dead. Struggling to speak, he burst out crying. He was his favourite uncle. The day came and before he could blink, the boy saw the train. "Ooh, this is it!"

He took a deep breath. Suddenly, the train came crashing straight into the boy.

"Woah!" said the man driving the train, as it crashed through countless people. One of them was the boy.

Taylan Branch (12)
Queen Katharine Academy, Walton

Alien Invasion

"Breaking news, alien ships are coming towards Earth, we have sent ships to make contact and they have been destroyed. We advise you to be prepared."
One week later and stores were completely empty and they were landing soon, I managed to get supplies and get into my underground bunker.
"Breaking news, the aliens are taking everyone as slaves, you should hide."
I came out two weeks later. They had left. I travelled the world and found around sixty people. We are going to repopulate the Earth. We are focusing on food at the moment. Two babies so far...

Alexandru Stan (14)
Queen Katharine Academy, Walton

Time Travel Trouble

I can't believe I have found Anne Boleyn's ancient necklace. I have used the scientific scanner I made and it's true!
I've been waiting to use my time travel machine. This is the perfect opportunity! I need to go back to the 16th century. Hopefully, it works. Strange, how did I find it on the ground? After preparing and updating the machine, it's finally complete – my next invention. As I enter, I switch the timelines and I arrive! It works! I need to go to the castle. I find some tools in my pockets. These may be useful. Hopefully, this goes well!

Fatima Gaye (13)
Queen Katharine Academy, Walton

Animopholia

I'm outside, hiding behind a bunch of trees in my backyard, crying, shaking and scared. I thought this kind of stuff was all made up by some stupid scientists who lied for some stupid attention or popularity. I was so, so wrong.

I hear growling and chewing. My mum, dad and brother are dead. Apparently, scientists have found some diseases from a plant that has never been discovered before. This plant is eaten by animals and causes them to deform and become gross, horrifying creatures, like skinwalkers.

Some horse-like creature is just eating my family... I'm doomed.

Tendai Mukurunge (13)
Queen Katharine Academy, Walton

The End Of The World

Lorrain saw something in the distance, something she hadn't seen before. Something extraordinary, dangerous, daring to even go near. She sprinted across the field to a wide road. However, there were no cars, no people, no life. Nothing. The earth began shaking. It growled and roared until a crack appeared. The earth shook from side to side getting faster by the second, as the crack grew larger. Then it broke. The earth crumbled at the end of the road. She took a step closer until her feet were on the edge of the world. Don't fall, don't do anything. Don't...

Leah Knappert (14)
Queen Katharine Academy, Walton

Foggy Season

Two years have flown by since the start of The Fog! The world used to be normal. Suddenly and swiftly, the grounds in Asia shattered open with gas that was foggy, it was named 'The Fog'. Scientists believe it's a natural phenomenon of highly toxic gas from the Earth's core. The people do not believe that. The research labs were raided and wiped out. It's a blood-red fog, when dense it turns black. Some call it 'Death's Breath'. When Death's Breath is inhaled the victim stops breathing instantaneously. That's how my brother died.

Jaden Swaby (15)
Queen Katharine Academy, Walton

My Life Changed With One Letter

One letter changed everything.
I was in my room with a book in my hand when someone knocked on the door. I went out to check who it was. My dad opened the door. A man handed him a letter. "Victoria!" My dad called my name. I rushed downstairs to get the letter from him. "It's for you." He gave the letter to me. I opened it up. I steadily read the first paragraph and it changed my life. I dropped the letter.
"What's the matter?" Dad said.
"I have to go to a concentration camp. We all have to..."

Andaleeb Hootak (12)
Queen Katharine Academy, Walton

The Aliens Invading Planet Earth

"Breaking news, the Prime Minister has declared an interesting sighting of what appears to be a UFO! It was as big as a dozen clouds with flashing lights of greens and reds. CCTV had barely captured lime-green bodies and ebony eyes. These creatures were... Argh!"

Uh oh, I thought as the ship had crashed on top of his building. "What am I going to do?" I whispered while pacing up and down my room. The Prime Minister was dead and it was me next. As crystal-clear tears rolled down my face, I heard a jet, a rescue helicopter!

Maisey Linnane (12)
Queen Katharine Academy, Walton

The Disaster Of New Year's Eve

On New Year's Eve, there were lots of deaths because of failed fireworks. The next day there was heavy rain and loud thunder and the roads were flooded and people were drowning. It felt like the world was ending every day for the past few weeks, there was a tornado and it destroyed so many neighbourhoods. The news was saying that the days were getting worse and worse. My whole family was worried and we tried going to a different country but the weather was so bad that every flight was cancelled.
One week later the weather started getting better.

Eduard Francu (12)
Queen Katharine Academy, Walton

He's The Only One Left

He was the only one left in the tight, scary, pitch-black cave.
There were small spiders dancing along the walls and a
scream as noisy as a dinosaur that never stopped. The
strong smell of dirt and dead bodies lingered all throughout
the cave. The more the scared, fragile boy walked, the
darker it got. One step and two steps, and then *boom!* He
was falling down a large hole like a deflated balloon. The
poor child screamed and wriggled around, crashing on the
walls of this massive hole. Tears filled his eyes whilst falling,
and he felt lifeless.

Sophie Longland (13)
Queen Katharine Academy, Walton

The End For Humanity

The news hit sooner than we ever expected. People were coming back from the grave. It seemed impossible to all, but that was before the pandemic hit. Everyone thought it'd just end, all quick and easy too. How much I desired that to be true. Before our eyes, the dead rose from their graves and bit the flesh of the innocent and they wouldn't stop... And now I'm the only one left from this mess. That's a mess in itself. I miss everyone. I wish this zombie doom would pass as if it was just all a terrible nightmare that I can't wake...

Sofia Alves (14)

Queen Katharine Academy, Walton

Demon Slayer: Cruelty

It was a good day until the smell of blood was uncovered. I climbed down the mountain to find an old man telling me it was not safe. "Why?" I asked.
"Demons," he replied. He shoved me into his house. Everyone in the village knows him as a good guy though, so I didn't question it. I just slept. When I woke up, I went straight home. Then I saw them, my whole family was slaughtered. Shocked, I checked my family's pulse, only my sister survived. I then swore to protect my sister and slay those demon scum. Blade to neck.

Stanley Snelling (12)
Queen Katharine Academy, Walton

War Is Not Impossible

My phone lights up with a buzz. I groan and roll over on my mattress. I rub my eyes and grab it.

My sleepy eyes grow wide as I read the contact, Lia – my sister. Oh no. This can't be happening. "Alica, it's true. It's really happening."

I shake my head and bury my buzzing phone into my duvet. "No, she's lying! A war is impossible," I try to reassure myself. I curl up into my bed as tears roll down my cheeks. It goes quiet. Too quiet. *Boom.*

Oh... There it was. The proof... A bomb...

Phoebe Craig (13)
Queen Katharine Academy, Walton

The Purge

I was just sitting on my bed, scrolling through my phone until suddenly, a siren went off. I was confused, as it wasn't my fire alarm or an alarm on my phone. The siren was loud and came from all directions. The sound of it was making my ears ring and I shot up from my bed, looking around. Words came from the siren saying, "Warning. The annual purge has begun. That means all activity, including murder, will be legal for twenty-four hours. Any medical services will not be available until 12pm tomorrow. May God be with you all."

Heidi Munton (12)
Queen Katharine Academy, Walton

Captured

Strange beings overwhelmed the planet. Two months ago, they took over our screens. They were tall and deformed, taking the appearance of a human bug. I was hiding out with my mother and sister. Their ship crashed into our neighbourhood. It was massive and the green smoke was still leaking out. I was caught while searching for food. The dry scaly skin grabbed me. I was terrified. Taking me to the ship, I was fed. I thought they were kind until I was thrown into the green goo. It was in my lungs. I couldn't breathe. They watched me suffocate.

Madison Dickson (14)
Queen Katharine Academy, Walton

The Letter That Changed My Life

I got a letter in the post today. I opened it up. I saw the name of the school. It was my university results. I didn't get in! I studied so hard for that!

I told my parents. They were so disappointed with me. It was like everyone was now disappointed with me! *Am I a failure?* I thought to myself... Yes, I was a failure!

All of a sudden, the ground started shaking. My bedroom was full of things that were flying everywhere. I was holding onto my window's handle. Would it get worse? Well, how could it get any worse?

Lily McCullough (12)
Queen Katharine Academy, Walton

It Had Only Been A Dream

Today, I was watching a movie then suddenly, the breaking news came on saying that the UK is going into a lockdown. They didn't say what reason for the lockdown, but as I was thinking, I heard police sirens all around the city with people in hazmat suits walking around the city. There was also a lot of fog even though it was sunny outside. In the distance, I saw smoke rising from the nuclear power plant. I thought: *history repeating.* I thought that I was stuck in Chernobyl, but suddenly, I woke up and saw it was only a dream.

Nikita Ignatovic (12)
Queen Katharine Academy, Walton

Sally

I was driving home from work. It had been a long day and I couldn't wait to get home and rest. I began to pull into the driveway. It felt different. Darker... Almost... dangerous!
I entered my home, ignoring the eerie feeling as I turned on the lights and walked into the kitchen. I saw a strange note on the counter. Despite the nasty feeling in my gut, I picked it up. It had some sort of sticky red substance on it. I was careful not to touch it.
As I read the note, it said, 'Sally's coming'.
Bang!

Stevie-Rose Keller (12)
Queen Katharine Academy, Walton

Alien Invasion

It all started on April 22nd at 8pm. The TV turned on and the President was talking, "Hide in your houses. Don't go outside." I looked out my window and saw that the sky was full of UFOs and other weird spaceships. You could see people being taken and killed by green alien species. It was chaos in Chicago. The military sent armies to take out the aliens. Most were successful but others were not so lucky. They were only able to take out two flocks of the alien ships until they were all gone, reduced to atoms. It was hell!

Liam Wright (14)
Queen Katharine Academy, Walton

The Small Storm

The lights went off. The storm was getting worse. Everyone was waiting until it got light again. It was 1pm but it wasn't light, it still looked like it was night. There were lights flickering, wires hissing. The storm had been going on for three days, nonstop. There was no internet. Nothing, except the dark and the candles we were using to see. People were running out of things to do, so they would go into the storm and stay there. The storm was gone. Two days later the clouds cleared up and the sun was brighter than usual...

Daniela Freimane (14)
Queen Katharine Academy, Walton

The Curer

Once the apocalypse started everybody had already boarded up their houses, but some decided to try to steal from shops or other houses. Now, being the last one around it's been a year in this new world, although knowing I'm the last one I feel like I'm being watched at all times. Scientists had worked on a cure, I now have it but I have not used it as the zombies don't come out during the day, but tonight's the night. Trap set up and zombies coming. No zombies came, they became smarter then slipped the trap.

Roman Levett (13)

Queen Katharine Academy, Walton

When Day Breaks

Remember when our parents told us to go outside? Well, now it's the opposite. The sky is red, the sun grows and now people and animals are turning into blobs of flesh that are bloodthirsty.

In the first hour, 90% of the population has fallen to the sun. For me, it has reached night, so I go outside with a pistol in hand and I try to find better shelter before day. Then, I see a large blob chasing me. I see an IKEA and enter.

Then, I hear something. "The store is now closed. Please exit the building."

Zachary Terry (12)
Queen Katharine Academy, Walton

Nuclear

August 21, 2040, 1:30am, life changed for the worst. Sludge reeking of radiation, fires burning, people screaming in pure agony. Pure chaos. If only people listened to me when I said reactor four was too hot to handle. But they didn't and now I'm stuck here, vomiting blood and coughing my lungs out. All I can hear is sirens, screaming and raging fires. All I can see is gas and my blood. All I can feel is my skin melting off from the inside out. All I can think about is my family. I know at this moment, I am trapped.

Amelia Keeble (14)
Queen Katharine Academy, Walton

The Virus

Another day in hell, we've been sectioned off from the rest of the world. Cities overtaken by nature, this is the last safe place on Earth. If you're stupid enough to go out there you absolutely have to wear a gas mask and be careful of them. They used to be people but the virus has taken over their bodies and turned them into creatures. They lurk in the dark, waiting for their victims. No one has ever survived a trip out to no man's land. Hmmm, what's that sound? A siren? No, it can't be, oh god, no!

Jacob Isack (14)
Queen Katharine Academy, Walton

The Crash

I was the only one left.

"Come on, we're going to be late," my mum yelled up the stairs as we all grabbed our coats and headed to the driveway.

The journey was around three hours, we drove at a slow pace. I noticed a black van behind us most of the journey, if only I had paid more attention.

It was foggy that day, the light rain patted on the roof of the car.

"I need gas," said Dad as we came to a stop on the side of the road. I got out to catch my breath.

Crash!

Zoha Zahra (12)
Queen Katharine Academy, Walton

The Worst Day Of My Life

I was having the worst day ever. My nan had given me and my cousins tickets to Alton Towers for Christmas. We were over the moon. We got in the car, drove halfway there and ran out of fuel. We went to the gas station and filled it up. We carried on driving. We got there and dropped all of our stuff. We got to the entrance. "Tickets please." We looked in my bag. They weren't there. My cousins called our nan. They weren't in the car. We checked our pockets. They were nowhere to be found. We were doomed.

Gracie Baines (12)
Queen Katharine Academy, Walton

The Scream

Lights went dark, screaming in the rooms around, then silence. Jones crawled across the room, trying not to make a single sound. He was limited in his movement as his leg got slashed by glass. The door slammed open with a spine-chilling breeze. The mutated ran in fast. Jones got up and ran to the closest room. The mutated closely followed behind. Jones made it outside, and there was no one to be seen. Cars abandoned, fires everywhere. At that moment, Jones knew that it was the end of the world. So he sat, distraught.

Harvey Townsend (14)
Queen Katharine Academy, Walton

The Flash Flood

A girl called Sarah was sitting alone in the living room watching TV when the news came on. The reporter said a flash flood was about to happen. Sarah went to tell her mum and dad, but they didn't believe her until an alert came up on their phones. They packed backpacks and went up to the attic, but her dad couldn't close the latch in time, and the water started to catch up to them. They climbed onto the roof and waited for help. Five whole hours later, they had eaten all the food, then a helicopter came.

Summer Turney (12)
Queen Katharine Academy, Walton

The World War

It was a normal day. I woke up, went downstairs and made my breakfast. After I finished, I sat down and put the news on, and that's when I heard it, there was a World War: Humans vs Robots. The news was telling us about how they created their own language. I heard a knock at my door. I checked the cameras, and robots broke in. I grabbed a machete, stabbed one in the head and struggled to fight the other four. I managed to escape. I found a plane and flew away. They were shooting at it. I finally escaped.

Mohammed Shamoun (14)
Queen Katharine Academy, Walton

Losing My Phone

"Where did I put it?" I just want to change the song while I clean my room. I need to look for it. How did it go missing? It was just on my bed a minute ago when I checked. Wait, let me ask someone to help me find it. Why does everyone have to be busy? I have looked everywhere. I can't find it. "Yay!" I hear my phone ringing. It must be under my pillows. It's not under them but I hear it ringing over this side of my room. Wait. Yes! It's inside my pillowcase. Finally!

Shania Hogan (13)
Queen Katharine Academy, Walton

Unknown

One day, I had to have an injection, however, there were some side effects. There was a really rare one called Unknown. After I had the injection, everything went bad. When I got home my mum told me my dad had left. A couple of hours later my dog died. I thought my day couldn't get any worse when I fell down the stairs and then realised I had got Unknown from the injection. Then I realised I was him. I was that 1%. When I got in the shower my hair fell out, I was bald. Later on, my mum died.

Ebrima Lowe (13)
Queen Katharine Academy, Walton

My Hair Disappeared

I was sleeping soundly, dreaming about doing my hair in the morning. Hearing a buzz sound near my hair tingling it, I put my hands on my head to feel not my luscious, soft curls, but nothing! A clean shave met my hands in shock. I dashed up out of my bed, fearing the worst. Was my hair gone? Please let this be a nightmare. I sprinted to a mirror in fear and saw what I thought was the impossible. My nightmare became a reality, my hair was gone and I was bald. I fainted and fell into a long coma.

Ubayd Hassan (14)
Queen Katharine Academy, Walton

War

Breaking news, the Prime Minister has ordered everyone to evacuate from high places because there is a war coming. As you know, there has been war in Ukraine and Israel. Sadly, the war has spread across the world. People are being warned about this. We think that there are attack planes coming for us. So, people, run as fast and as far as you can, or else you will die. I have been told that there are trucks coming to help those who can't help themselves. There are camps you can go to.

Nyasha Manyeruke (13)
Queen Katharine Academy, Walton

A Raging Tornado Taking Over London

As soon as the news warned everyone about this deadly storm, the internet went out. The heavy wind was taking control over the city and the raindrops were gushing down. All I could hear were the screams of London and how hard my heart was pumping. As I looked outside, all I saw was a huge tornado rushing towards me. Within a heartbeat, I rushed to get my belongings and leave. As soon as I got my stuff I ran to the door and opened it. The rain was gushing down. I looked around, I woke up.

Benas Benesevicius (13)
Queen Katharine Academy, Walton

I Lost My Phone

I was chilling on my bed. My phone was on charge. The table was shaking and then my phone disappeared. There was a portal flowing through the oven. When I went in there, I was teleported to a snow biome. I was walking until I stumbled across a house. It was horrifying until I went through the rotting door. I saw my phone behind my parents. They were stuck to a chair and when I went to free them, they changed into alien dogs and kept biting me until I woke up. Phew! It was just a dream.

Helvan Ali (12)
Queen Katharine Academy, Walton

Ruins

A great fire, unlike the fire of London, it was much bigger.
More destruction, more deaths. The city was left in ruins,
buildings burnt to a crisp and cars exploded. Little to no
survivors. The city was left in shambles, and by the time it
was over the skyscrapers had collapsed, this catastrophic
incident was worldwide with the most fire spreading all
around. Habitats, forests, jungles and more had been
demolished. It was pure destruction caused by climate
change and global warming.

Matas Karčiauskas (13)
Queen Katharine Academy, Walton

Losing My Phone

Where did it go? I was already having the worst day ever and now I was having bad luck, starting with losing my phone. I remembered putting it on the table in my room and the next thing I knew, it was gone! I looked everywhere in my room but no one had seen it. I asked my mum to help me look for it around the house and then... After searching for what felt like hours, we finally found it. It somehow was in my room under the covers. It made my day better knowing I finally found it.

Kotryna Krutkeviciute (13)

Queen Katharine Academy, Walton

The Bombs Flood

The war was happening. People screaming. People crying for help. Then there was silence. I was confused, but then someone was screaming. I was confused again, but then I smelled smoke. I heard a baby cry so I ran to the crying baby, but the whole room was on fire. Then I saw five bombs flying in the sky. I picked up the baby and ran out of the room as fast as I could, but when I went outside the apartment more bombs were outside, like a bomb flood. So I found an underground base.

Hollie Westgarth (13)
Queen Katharine Academy, Walton

Day Of The Poor

I have just received the most devastating, heartbreaking and depressing news of my whole, long, healthy life. Why did this just happen to me? Am I going poor? My whole entire life has changed. Will people miss me when I'm out? I have to deliver agonising news, but now this isn't even possible. I feel scared as if something's going to happen to me. Can I even help myself? If you're confused about what I'm talking about, my data ran out.

Jaela Graham (13)
Queen Katharine Academy, Walton

Eternal Darkness

The world isn't normal and hasn't been for a while. Nothing to do, but stare into the endless void. No fun, no family, no friends, no nothing. A spark of hope every now and again, that little light or spark to show up and free us. Free me. But for now, I sit in the void, to be forgotten, trapped and lost. A light comes around every now and again. It is my only company. To me, it's like my only family now. Forever in the void.

Doulton Coleman (12)
Queen Katharine Academy, Walton

Shellshock

I look out of my window to see a building swallowed in flames. A bomb drops, leaving my ears ringing and hurting. A sense of relief when I realise I'm not hit, then I see a flat is gone. I go down and open the door. I see empty bullet shells and stacks of corpses. I hear screaming. So I close the door quickly. I hear something breathing down my beck. I turn around and see a soldier, gun pointed straight at my head...

Alexandru Ciortan (13)
Queen Katharine Academy, Walton

Crazy Death

Today was the worst day ever. I was walking with my grandma near town before someone barged into her and she went up a ramp, she did six radical backflips in the air before getting bashed by a bus. I could hear her screams as she went flying into a river and drifted away. I remember getting an injection which had some side effects, one being unknown which made your life hell, and then I realised, I had it.

Blake Erskine (13)
Queen Katharine Academy, Walton

Creeps

Shadows dance in the moonlit halls. Whispers echo along the walls. Souls of the past, they softly tread. With phantom hands, it grasps for breath. A ghostly vow to welcome death. Through the dusk, it stalks its prey. Under veiled rooms, it claims its stay. Mysteries linger, dark and deep. In this house, where a spirit creeps.

Latham Fane (15)
Queen Katharine Academy, Walton

Weather Control

"Elizabeth," the NASA director said, "why does NASA need a geographical scientist?"
Elizabeth replied, "Wouldn't NASA like to control the weather, I can make that happen."
Elizabeth was hired and immediately got to work developing a formula that could control the weather. After a year it was done, Elizabeth mixed magnetised metal into the formula and dropped it into the ocean. This makes the water controlled via gigantic magnets, however it had the opposite effect. Acid rain, it spread all over the world and killed almost everyone, and then it got into the water supply. No one was safe.

Zara Esat (12)
Raedan Institute, Leicester

Stuck

Everything went dark. I was stuck in the basement. I couldn't move and I couldn't eat. I only went to move some furniture, but I had forgotten that my family had gone shopping. I felt very lonely.

How could everyone forget about me?

I couldn't move at all, because I was stuck between two machines. I was so hungry, and I was so bored. I hoped my family would come quickly, so I could finally be free. Suddenly, I heard something upstairs, so I screamed for help. The door opened, but that face... I didn't recognise it.

Who was this? Why were they in my house?

Abdullah Motara (12)
Raedan Institute, Leicester

It's Just The End Of The World

Have you ever heard the saying, 'Keep your friends close, but keep your enemies closer'?

Samuel did and ended up in jail for suspicion of the murder of a man named Damion Winser. Then he had planned to end the world after successfully escaping jail.

In order to end the world, he set every single forest and woodland on fire. He kidnapped and killed.

No one, and I mean no one, could stop him. Not even his family.

Why you may ask?

All of this was because Damion sent him to the hospital for mentally ill people.

Whose fault was it?

Ruqayyah Abdurrahman (12)
Raedan Institute, Leicester

Stella, The Only Survivor Left

Stella was the only survivor left, who was once part of a helpful community. She had tried everything to keep the people alive, she even tried herbal hand-made medicine. Weeks quickly turned into months and slowly years. She was determined to never give up. Stella, the young girl, didn't know something really bad was coming ahead of her. One day, roaming around the forests late at night, she realised she was lost! "Oh no!" Young Stella was crowded by animals. She thought a rescue team or some people would save her, no one knows what happened next...

Sumaya Aden (11)
Raedan Institute, Leicester

Thick Smoke

The thick smoke was coming and the door I was near to wasn't opening. All of a sudden, everything went dark and the smoke was blocking my airways. I ripped the radiator off the wall and, after multiple hits on the wooden door, it burst open. It was almost impossible to see anything as the smoke enveloped me tearing up my eyes. The exit was flashing green and the loud screeching of the bell rang in my ears, nearly bursting my eardrums. I finally made my way through the harsh debris but when I reached the door it too was jammed. My heart stopped.

Ahmed Taylor (12)
Raedan Institute, Leicester

Deadly Virus

Breaking news, the Prime Minister has declared that a deadly virus is spreading at a fast speed and every minute that's passing, thousands of people are passing away and at this rate, the end of the human population is getting closer. If scientists don't find a cure for it then it will probably be the end of the world. People who have the virus know they are going to die and they're trying not to contaminate anyone. When the virus comes to a country rich people emigrate to another country and it is as if they are playing tag with it.

Ilyes Boutefennouchet (14)
Raedan Institute, Leicester

The Meteor

Breaking news, the Prime Minister has declared that a meteor will hit. I can't believe this is how I die. I am only fifteen. I don't want to die like this. I have to do something to stop it. I speak to my dad. He says he works with people who can help. I ask him to take me so we can try to survive. We drive. Then I go in. Dad greets everyone. We speak to them. They say they can't do anything. We sit there and watch the big screen. Five, four, three, two, one, I mutter under my breath as the bright meteor hits.

Muhammad Ismael Katib (13)
Raedan Institute, Leicester

Mission Catastrophe

One day, a cat was announced as missing. But on the same day, it was said that after that incident, a cat got run over by a truck. It was said that the cat that died was the same colour as the missing cat. So the owner thought her cat died and lived on. But... two years later a cat was spotted, it looked exactly like the missing cat. But the owner thought it was impossible. Until... she saw the cat in her garden and she knew it was her. The cat went in and they were happily united once again.

Inaya Chevalier (11)
Raedan Institute, Leicester

The Camping Trip

My friends and I were on a camping trip, when we decided to go for a walk in the woods. We saw many different animals. Before night started to fall we headed back to our camp, until we realised we were lost. Every direction looked the same. We decided to set up camp where we were, then ate some food and after our meal we dozed off. A couple of days passed, we knew we couldn't stay there forever. So we took a risk and followed a random path and, surprisingly, we made it back to our city.

Amaan Chevalier

Raedan Institute, Leicester

The Town Gone Wrong

It was a Thursday and my mum had just told me that we were going to London to visit Grandma. I was so excited because I hadn't seen Grandma in over a year.

Mum booked the train and the next day we woke up early. I packed my bag and got in the car, and we drove to the train station. We were waiting for our train, but it came late, so Mum went to get snacks from the vending machine. Finally, the train came. I got on and to my shock, I saw my mum chasing the train.

Abdulraheem Katib (12)

Raedan Institute, Leicester

Was It You All Along?

Am I the only one left? The devastating plague's rapid spread led to a terrifying transformation, with infected individuals turning into zombies!
I wished none of this had ever happened, the accident that changed everything, the secret that tore us apart. My brother Marc's sudden disappearance raised suspicions about the dark secrets he may be hiding. As I deciphered the cryptic message on his old photograph, a chilling realisation struck me. The mystery surrounding Marc deepened, leaving me questioning, was it truly him all along? The uncertainty loomed large as I grappled with the haunting possibility of the brother I thought I knew.

Nicole Kaldas (14)
Sacred Heart High School, Hammersmith

Untitled

Tears. They were streaming down my face. One text changed everything. Why? Why would he do that? Leaving me here - irate and desolate. I never meant for this to happen. *Ring, ring.* I felt the vibration of the phone. It was Lucas. Before I could even stop myself, I answered. "Babe, let me exp-"

"No! You and I could've been something. But you never wanted that, did you?" I screamed down the phone aggressively.

"I-I-"

"How could you use me?"

Silence. Silence filled my minute bedroom. My phone had died. Drained, like my soul. Trapped by my own emotions.

Daisy Inyundo (11)
Sacred Heart High School, Hammersmith

The Countdown

I approached my workplace, ready to start another day of work, when I glimpsed a peculiar red light above me. My head whipped around, then froze, as I tried to fathom what I'd witnessed. A countdown had commenced.

Panic began to cloud my wretched thoughts, screaming at one man as the answer. Frantic, I sprinted towards my neighbour's house, racing the countdown as it reached its final seconds. I pounded on the door, breathless. As the door opened, I yelled out, "How dare you! You're the one responsible for this..."

I was now surrounded by a chocolate sprinkle haven. "Disaster."

Bethel Kebede (13)

Sacred Heart High School, Hammersmith

Corruption

I stand astray, lost in despair. Shaking, the tingling sensation down my spine. I tremble falling on my knees in tears of regret. Everything destroyed... utterly corrupted, because of me. We started in unity; solo I am now. The cries of joy turned into horrific screams. I released the crazed demon that once was sealed and now it's come back for another meal. Annihilated humanity. If only I could turn back time to change the inevitable. And now I go down in history as the embodiment of greed; the *'villain'* who made the world suffer a cruel fate.

Nia Fletcher-Anderson (12)
Sacred Heart High School, Hammersmith

Survival Of The Fittest

A harsh slam against the floor sounded through the blaring sirens as the ceiling collapsed - a vivid scarlet light engulfing the endless hallway. It was only because of a blood-curdling scream, that I pivoted to look behind me. With an arm out, my friend on the floor pleaded for me to help her out of the rubble which collapsed over her foot and held her prisoner. My eyes darted frantically between her, and the rest of the evacuees who were sprinting down the corridor - heart drumming against my chest.
"Sorry," I choked out, before turning away to run.

Carmen Zmudzka-Chung (14)
Sacred Heart High School, Hammersmith

Two-Pound Sandwich

It was any normal day flying over the rich Amazon rainforest with my cheap two-pound sandwich in hand. I was living the life. Then suddenly a frantic announcement over the speaker. "Mayday mayday, the plane is going down. Brace yourselves." I froze, I couldn't move, then suddenly the plane began to tip. I heard screams and cries, phone calls being made and then silence. The flight attendants telling everyone to keep calm and hope for the best. I was the only one listening, I was the only one calm. Then no more screams, no cries. Just complete silence.

Hannah Scully Martin (12)
Sacred Heart High School, Hammersmith

Untitled

I darted through the paved streets of London. Sweat trickled down my face and onto my shirt. People fell, gripping their throats, blood pouring from their mouths, their eyeballs popping out as if there were springs behind them. I clutched the small bubbling beaker of green liquid in a tight fist. I had to get to the hospital. It would stop this dreadful plague before it spread out of London. The air was stuffy and smelt of death. My breath was getting slower and shallower. Oh no! I poured the liquid down my throat. Then I remembered: "Only one drop."

Sofia Carvalho-Hunt (12)
Sacred Heart High School, Hammersmith

Tick-Tock Goes The Clock Before You Lose Your Mind

In the dimly lit room, shadows danced across the walls as his mind spiralled into chaos. His eyes once vibrant, now held a vacant stare. Every creak of the floorboards echoed in his ears, amplifying the whispers that plagued his thoughts. The world blurred around him as he lost touch with reality, trapped in a labyrinth of his own making. His laughter, tinged with madness, filled the air as he surrendered to the darkness within. Sanity slipped away, like sand through his trembling fingers, leaving behind a man lost in the depths of his own madness.

Tessa Hogan (14)
Sacred Heart High School, Hammersmith

The Boy Who Could Destroy The World

This adolescent boy could destroy the world. And he didn't even know it. How he unearthed the formula is a mystery to all. The mere mention of it was enough to make everyone uneasy - a taboo subject. None dared to speak up as if the matter of a young boy able to eradicate the whole human race wasn't an already pressing matter to confer.

There was only one question to ask. Unspoken, yet everybody knew it. Unreachable, if only one could grasp it. "How can we hide this boy from the world when he knows to destroy it?"

Eira-Geen Cauilan (12)

Sacred Heart High School, Hammersmith

Earth Shatters

Theo looked out the window, waiting for the dawn sky to clear. The sky was purple and black, winds swirling loudly, then Theo knew something was not right. Thunder rumbled and rocks fell through the sky. He knew what was happening; he had read about it in space books. The Earth was shattering! He ran out of the house and gazed at the rocks falling around him. He knew that it wasn't safe, but he had to see what was happening. Then the Earth collapsed, and he was falling through space, stars gleaming at him till the world went black.

Anna Rizzato (11)
Sacred Heart High School, Hammersmith

Miranda Hatchcock

The thick smoke was choking me. I was dying. Hello, my name is Miranda Hatchcock, I am 80 years old. I couldn't believe it, I was about to die I could try running, but I couldn't run that fast. I could try to hide but the fire would eventually catch me. I didn't know what there was to do. There was no one around me to save me. I might as well just try and run. I started to run. I ran faster and faster. The fire was spreading faster and faster. I couldn't breathe anymore. That's me done forever.

Rosa Barrett (11)

Sacred Heart High School, Hammersmith

The Prank

I didn't mean for this to happen. It was supposed to be funny, not disastrous. Everything was muddled up in front of me; Mr Redthorn rushed to hospital, my teacher sending us to the head, yet the only thing I focused on was that I was one of them now, one of the popular girls. I went up to them, hopeful, but they shoved me aside. "You messed it up. It wasn't supposed to end like this!" they shouted. They warned me that if I ever said a word that they ordered me to do it I would regret it...

Jaya Sharma (12)
Sacred Heart High School, Hammersmith

One Text Changed Everything!

I was on my way to school and everyone was staring at...
me! I sauntered inside and people were gossiping about this
text that I had sent so I went and scrutinised, but the one
boy that I had a crush on for an eternity was actually
looking at me with a galled look on his face! I was
wondering what I did and I thought I would keep mute for
now until I comprehended that it was the text I sent to the
most popular girl in the school, that one girl that bullied me!

Lola Pasin (11)

Sacred Heart High School, Hammersmith

The Last One Left

Everything went dark. It was a bitter cold, stormy night and the wind was howling aggressively. I was the last one left. I knew it was a bad idea to walk in the misty forest alone late at night but it was too late to go back.

Suddenly, sounds of faint footsteps became louder and louder and louder until I turned around and I couldn't believe my eyes! A masked figure holding a mysterious weapon stood right in front of me. I did not dare to move...

Teresa Lo (12)
Sacred Heart High School, Hammersmith

Boom!

I didn't mean for this to happen, I really didn't... How would I have known that clicking a button on the microwave would make it explode? Like, I saw on TikTok that if you microwave a grape, it will taste really good and that 'totally nothing bad will happen'. I wish I had paid attention in science, it'd probably prevent that from happening.
Life lesson; never microwave a grape again!

Gabriela Hanna (12)

Sacred Heart High School, Hammersmith

A Trial Of Tribulations

Yet somehow more deafening than thunder. Her eyes were blindfolded. She was tightly strapped to a chair, her arms bound behind her. And yet. She could feel their deprecating stares boring holes into her flesh, a hunger drowning her like an insurmountable ocean. A hunger, to be satiated by the finale of a grand performance. Anticipation. The resounding bang of the gavel echoes through the court-like hall. "The verdict." A pause.

"I declare the souls of those on Earth..." The air was practically boiling with an almost tangible feverishness.

"...Guilty."

"The sentence."

"Complete annihilation." She would die.

Olivia Arthur (14)
St Margaret's School For Girls, Aberdeen

A Night To Remember

"You're early," says Death. "What happened?"

"She pushed me-"

Giggles waltzed above the dance floor. I shot upstairs, elbowing starched shirts and brilliant jewels, straining to hear her. Maria sounded happy - sounded *free*. Old tears threatened to spill over. Our gazes met. String lights exposed the softening of her expression - the pity in her eyes. A wave of grief rocked me into her arms. Maria flinched away from my touch, striking my chest.

And now, Death comforts me. "She wasn't supposed to go to prom without you."

I try to stifle a sob, but the shattered bones do not move.

Abigail Onyeakazi (15)

St Margaret's School For Girls, Aberdeen

Just Like Me

She was staring at me, her gaunt figure jerked uncontrollably as her breath quickened.
In. Out. In. Out.
The two of us stared into our similarly glassy eyes.
There was a *jarring* reason for our similarities.
That girl was me.
I remembered looking at my reflection in the puddle near my folks' yard. She was staring right back at me... until she wasn't. She started shaking, screaming, and speaking a language I didn't understand. While I sat *completely still.*
All I remembered was her pale hand pulling me under the water, and her slurring lips saying, "We found her."

Clarissa Iluore (13)

St Margaret's School For Girls, Aberdeen

The Earth Is Dead

It's dead silent - except for the occasional scream from the burning streets outside, as a feral dog catches another victim, and my finger tapping 'SOS' on the homemade transmitter. I don't know how or why the ozone layer collapsed. I do, however, know I'm going to die unless someone hears my signal. My stomach aches with hunger, thirst and despair. The heat in this wardrobe (my hideout for the last month) is stifling. I tap out the code for what seems like the hundredth time that day, no longer requiring the Morse code guide. Nothing. Again. Then... four dots, two dots... "Hi".

Lucinda Kerr (12)
St Margaret's School For Girls, Aberdeen

The Permanent Swap

It was a beautiful day with lots of sunshine and a clear blue sky. The Yelnats family constantly has bad luck, so their family outings are usually ruined, even though this time of year is ideal for them to spend quality time together and *nothing will go wrong!*

They used to go shopping and enjoy ice cream on days like today. Everything was going surprisingly well, they enjoyed a shared bowl of banana split ice cream after their incredible shopping spree. They returned home, and little did they know that they would change their lives forever. They all swapped bodies.

Akshaya Allagappan (12)
St Margaret's School For Girls, Aberdeen

Hidden Viruses

Ignoring the warnings, I downloaded the update. A flicker of light flashed across the sky. I scanned it in anticipation. *This was the new update, wasn't it?*

What once had been a setting sunset, was now a black swirling vortex. I glanced down at my phone and lurched back, the former glow of the screen was replaced with a hooded figure beginning to rise from its inside: green lines coursing throughout its cloak. It opened its mouth and a swirl of green numbers came crashing down upon me. I tore the goggles from my eyes. *What was going on?*

Thejal Senthil (11)

St Margaret's School For Girls, Aberdeen

Pink Thoughts

I read your diary after cleaning out your room. I didn't want Mum to know, she'd get too emotional. I never knew how much your friends loved you, or how many teachers adored you. We didn't talk much. Ever since I burned myself trying to pick up your diary that jerk burned, I have been getting these weird thoughts, like you would have had: how our parents didn't understand you, and how our brother annoyed you all day. Funny, how I'm the one writing the diary while you're just thoughts in my head. Bye sister, we loved you.
Love, Rafael.

Samaira Noor (13)
St Margaret's School For Girls, Aberdeen

Trapped

I slowly snatched my bag from the passenger seat noticing the driver was gone. My mind was spinning, *am I a hostage? Where am I?* I started kicking the car door open and sprinted through the vacant car park - and hit the forest. I heard the howling wind and piercing shrieks of the night animals. I forced my mind to keep going but my legs were thinking otherwise.

Suddenly I tripped on a branch of prickled thorns lying in front of me. I immediately started yelling in excruciating pain and despair but no one could hear me. I was trapped.

Pippa Stephen (12)
St Margaret's School For Girls, Aberdeen

The Corner Shop

Akshaya was a normal girl living a normal life until one day her life was flipped upside down.

Akshaya was walking home when she caught sight of a shop. It hadn't been there the other day, so where did it come from? Walking in, she suddenly realised it wasn't a shop, it was a trap!

The sky turned black as she plummeted to the ground and landed in a crumpled heap on the floor. After what seemed like forever, she struggled up and saw an uncanny lady standing over her. The lady smiled and said, "This is your home now."

Jenny Wang (12)
St Margaret's School For Girls, Aberdeen

It Changed Everything

Bill was at an exhibition centre and felt intrigued by one painting. It was a dodo. The eyes of the dodo would move if he moved.

Then a man came into view. He held out his hand.

Bill felt an uncanny bond with this man, so he followed him. In the distance, Bill saw a pinhead-sized blue dot. The man's red T-shirt started to bulge out and his skin turned green. Bill's hands seemed to reshape themselves and his nails turned into long claws. Little did he know he was transforming into an exotic alien - bit by bit.

Yazhini Kannan (12)
St Margaret's School For Girls, Aberdeen

The Glass Tree

The mirror shattered thousands of years ago, at a time when there was no going back. The world was cracked, the gods had died, and everything was put under a dark black mist. People have been slaving away since then, doing everything King Dovan ordered because if they didn't the black mist would suck the life out of them, leaving their bodies but eating their souls... However, there was a rip in time, a way to win the war that had been lost, once upon a time. All that had to be done was... to find the Glass Tree.

Aditi Krishna (13)
St Margaret's School For Girls, Aberdeen

The Glowing Fireball

The day was still. It was early and Aurora was getting ready - the sun was rising and the sky was bright. Aurora was ready to catch her school bus. As she sat down for her first class she looked outside and a huge orange fireball was flying through the sky. At first, she thought it was a rocket but it was something bigger and it was hurtling down! The fireball was getting closer... It was the sun! Everything went dark. Aurora fainted as the fireball hit the ground. She woke up years later to a shocking sight...

Faye Brown (13)
St Margaret's School For Girls, Aberdeen

Was I The Only One Left?

July 3002.

It was 2pm on a sweltering day in Hong Kong when I found myself walking next to a breathtaking pond. There was a burning temptation to jump in - a yearning as strong as the burning heat felt on my skin.

Suddenly, a little girl bolted towards the pond. I noticed all the ducks freezing as the girl jumped in; she seemed to descend lower and lower until she finally disappeared. When she resurfaced, I watched her as she was consumed, dissolved, and disappeared into the dense waters.

Yasmin Wiseman (12)

St Margaret's School For Girls, Aberdeen

The Day The Sun Didn't Rise

I will never forget this day. I finally woke up from a terrible nightmare, only to realise that I had entered the sequel of my night terrors. It felt like it was the first day that the sun had risen. But as my eyes began to focus, I realised it was not the sun that had come up. It was something much brighter, a piercing light that warned me to move no further. I had no choice. I had to stay put. I knew that death was looming - it was ominous - ready to catch me in its trap.

Lucy Cherrie (13)

St Margaret's School For Girls, Aberdeen

YOUNG WRITERS INFORMATION

We hope you have enjoyed reading this book – and that you will continue to in the coming years.

If you're a young writer who enjoys reading and creative writing, or the parent of an enthusiastic poet or story writer, do visit our website **www.youngwriters.co.uk**. Here you will find free competitions, workshops and games, as well as recommended reads, a poetry glossary and our blog.

If you would like to order further copies of this book, or any of our other titles, then please give us a call or visit **www.youngwriters.co.uk**.

Young Writers
Remus House
Coltsfoot Drive
Peterborough
PE2 9BF
(01733) 890066
info@youngwriters.co.uk

Join in the conversation!

f YoungWritersUK   **X** YoungWritersCW
⊙ youngwriterscw   **♪** youngwriterscw